This Book Belongs to...

_____

Crocodaddy

Crocodaddy

by Kim Norman

illustrated by David Walker

STERLING

New York / London

Library of Congress Cataloging-in-Publication Data Available

2 4 6 8 10 9 7 5 3 1

Published by Sterling Publishing Co., Inc.
387 Park Avenue South, New York, NY 10016
Text copyright © 2009 by Kim Norman
Illustrations copyright © 2009 by David Walker
The artwork was prepared using acrylics on heavy paper.
Designed by Scott Piehl and Jessica Dacher
Distributed in Canada by Sterling Publishing
c/o Canadian Manda Group, 165 Dufferin Street
Toronto, Ontario, Canada M6K 3H6
Distributed in the United Kingdom by GMC Distribution Services
Castle Place, 166 High Street, Lewes, East Sussex, England BN7 1XU
Distributed in Australia by Capricorn Link (Australia) Pty. Ltd.
P.O. Box 704, Windsor, NSW 2756, Australia

Sterling ISBN 978-1-4027-4460-0

For information about custom editions, special sales, premium and
corporate purchases, please contact Sterling Special Sales
Department at 800-805-5489 or specialsales@sterlingpublishing.com.

For Kelvin, our own

beloved Crocodaddy.

— K. N.

For our "croc-o-buddies,"

Matthew and Joseph.

— D. W.

Down in the pond by a mossy rock,
something slithers past the dock.
Minnows dart with startled jerks—
this is where the Crocodaddy lurks!

Safe behind the rock, I see
sly old **Crocodaddy**
smile at me.

Fearlessly, I step in front,
captain of the
Crocodaddy hunt!

Crocodaddy,
Crocodaddy,

swim away fast.
This day's swim
could be your last!

Out on the dock I look below.
Where'd that slippery Crocodaddy go?

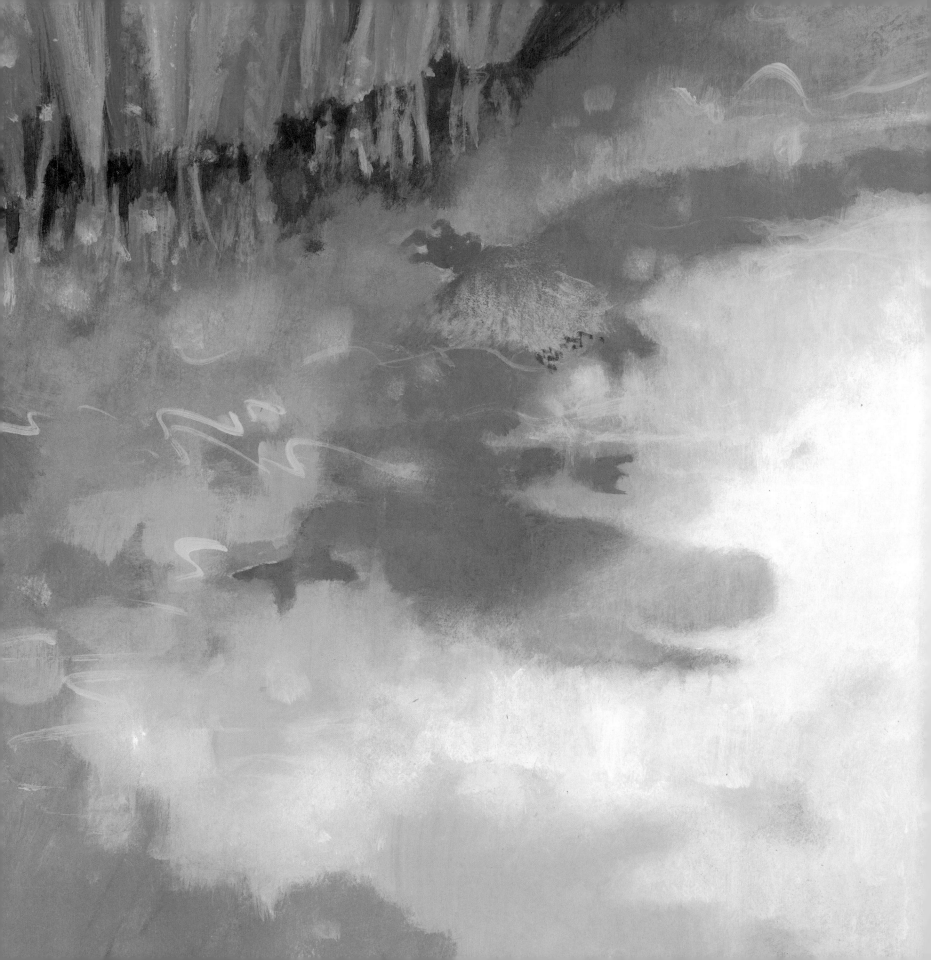

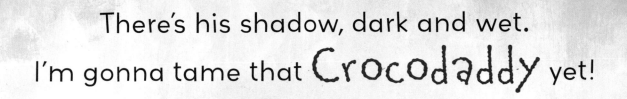

There's his shadow, dark and wet.
I'm gonna tame that Crocodaddy yet!

Tossing off my hat and pack ... HAAAAH!
I leap on Crocodaddy's back!

Crocodaddy, Crocodaddy,
whatcha gonna do?
Crocodaddy hunter is
RIDING on you!

Water sprays like crystal whips.
Crocodaddy rumbles bubbly lips.
Now he turns his head and winks.

Slowly, s l o w l y, Crocodaddy sinks!

Water rises ripply blue,
chills my laughing belly, too.

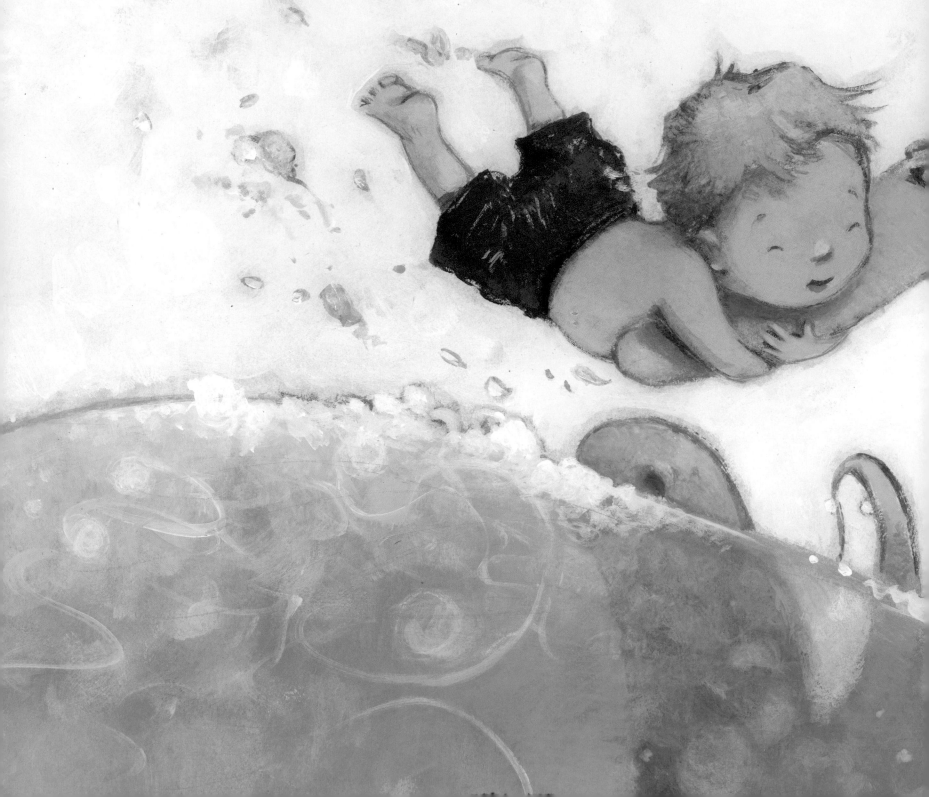

Even though he's STILL not tame,
holding tight, I shout his name . . .

Crocodaddy,
Crocodaddy,
can't get away!
I'm on top,
and here I'll stay!

'Round my knees, the water churns.
Splashing, thrashing, Crocodaddy turns,
whips up waves that slap the shore,
then lets out a Crocodaddy...

ROAR!

Such a roar that, oops—oh, no!

SPLASH!

I slip . . . and in I go!

Spitting water, now I see
hunting crocs is hard on ME!

Crocodaddy,
Crocodaddy,
just you wait.
You're gonna bite a
different bait.

Let's just give it one more try.

THIS time when he slithers by,

I discover something new:

Crocodaddy knees are ticklish, too!

THAT'S how you tame a
Crocodaddy pet ...

(you don't need a rope

and you don't need a net!)

Crocodaddy,
Crocodaddy,
lyin' on the dock—
and I'm a little chip
off the lazy old Croc!